בס"ד

This book belongs to:

לה׳ הארץ ומלואה

MORAH DEVORAH! ✰

Please read it to me!

Hachai

As Big as an Egg

A Story About Giving by: Rochel Sandman
Illustrated by: Chana Zakashanskaya

Hachai
PUBLISHING

Dedicated in memory of Bubbe Hinda by her Children & Grandchildren

❧

Dovid Shlomo & Sara Deitsch

❧

Mordechai & Brana Shaina Deitsch & Family
Joseph & Shterna Deitsch & Family
Rochel Leah & Yosef Tzvi Sandman & Family
Ella & Mayer Zeiler & Family
Chanah Devorah & Yankel Pinson & Family

❧

Zalman Deitsch, Avraham Moshe Deitsch,
Yosef Deitsch & Gavriel Gopin

❧

Rivkin, Gorowitz, Brook & Karp Families

To my husband Yosef Tzvi with thanks for all your encouragement and support. *R.S.*

❧

As Big as an Egg

First Edition: Elul 5755 / September 1995
Second Impression: Nissan 5759 / March 1999

Copyright © 1995 by **Hachai Publishing**
ALL RIGHTS RESERVED

Edited by: D. Rosenfeld and R. Herman
Layout: G. Eichorn

Library of Congress Catalog Card Number: 95-75434
ISBN # 0-922613-77-X

HACHAI PUBLISHING
156 Chester Avenue, Brooklyn, New York 11218
Tel: (718) 633-0100 Fax: (718) 633-0103
www.hachai.com

Printed in Hong Kong

• •

Bubbe - Grandmother   **Mitzvah** - Commandment
Hashem - G-d   **Shema** - "Hear O Israel" prayer

The night was cold.
The line was long.
Chaim was very tired after working all day.
He was very hungry as he waited and waited
to buy one small loaf of bread.

One small loaf of bread on Monday, one small loaf of
bread on Thursday — that was all that anyone could
buy years ago in Russia during the war.

Chaim, like everyone in the bread-line, had a special
card. In order to buy bread, he needed to show his card
at the bakery.
Finally it was his turn.
Chaim held out his bread card and got his loaf of bread.

Chaim was happy to be going home.
He wanted to eat a fresh piece of bread and to drink
some hot tea before he went to sleep.

As Chaim walked out of the bakery, he saw Bubbe Hinda. There she stood with her bulging sack. He tried to leave quickly before Bubbe Hinda could see him. But Bubbe Hinda did see Chaim.

She came over to him and asked, "Will you please give me a piece of your bread to bring to people who are sick? They don't have any bread because they are too sick to wait in line with their bread cards. Please put some of your bread in the sack."

Chaim was very, very hungry.
He wanted to eat all of his own little loaf of bread.
But Chaim couldn't say no to Bubbe Hinda.

Bubbe Hinda opened her sack.

Chaim looked inside and saw the many
little pieces of bread that other people
had given her.

From his own crusty loaf, Chaim pulled
off a piece of bread about as big as an
egg. With a little sigh, he dropped
it in the sack.

Bubbe Hinda smiled at Chaim.
She said, *"Zol zein tzu mitzvah."**

Chaim went home.
He was very hungry.
He felt a little sorry that he had given
away some of his bread.

* *Yiddish:* "May you merit to do more good deeds."

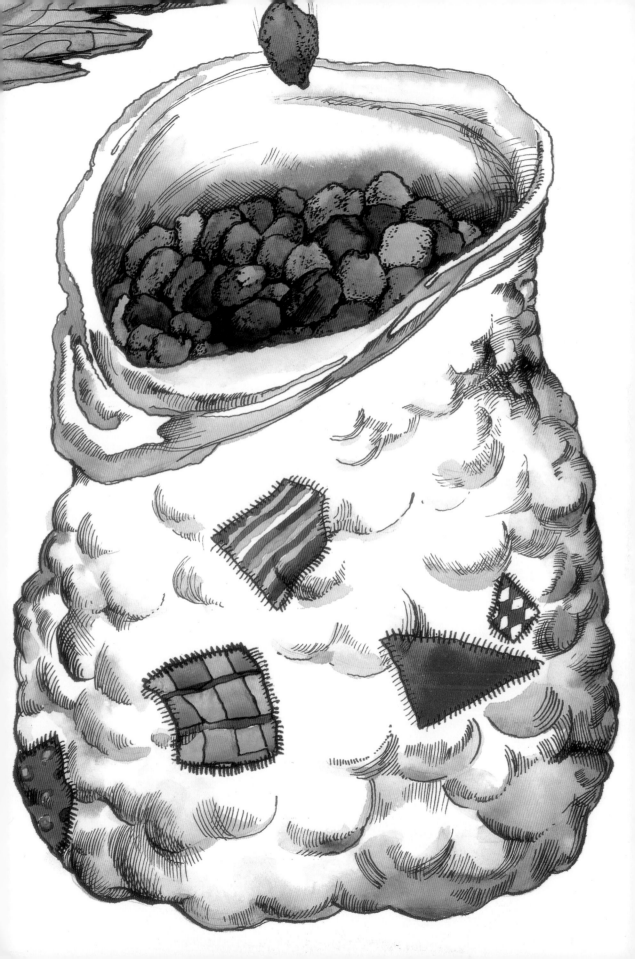

The next time Chaim was able to buy bread, he went to
a new bakery near his work. He held out his bread card.
He got his loaf of bread. Chaim clutched the crusty loaf
to his chest as he hurried home.

He was glad Bubbe Hinda was not there to ask him for bread to feed the sick people. He was glad that he had all of his bread for himself.

At home, Chaim washed his hands. He pulled off one chunk of fresh bread and said the blessing. He took tiny bites of bread and sipped his tea slowly to make his little meal last longer.

After thanking Hashem for the food, Chaim wrapped up
the rest of his bread, said *Shema* and went to sleep.

The next day, when Chaim came home from work—

He thought he heard a scurrying sound.

He thought he saw something run
into a hole in the wall.

He thought he saw the tip of a tail
shake like a scolding finger.

Chaim took out his bread and found that a piece
was missing, a piece about **as big as an egg** !

Chaim was very annoyed.
He looked around the room and closed up all the holes
he could find. Then he washed his hands and sat down
to eat his bread and drink his tea.
"I must be more careful with my bread next time,"
Chaim said to himself.

In a few days, Chaim came home from the new bakery
with another loaf of bread. He ate his meal. Then he
wrapped his bread carefully and put it away on the
highest shelf in the house. Now his bread was safe.

Chaim smiled as he said *Shema* and went to sleep.

When Chaim came home from work the
next night —

He thought he heard a scurrying sound.

He thought he saw something run by.

He thought he saw the tip of a tail
shake like a scolding finger.

Chaim pulled down his bread from the
shelf and saw that a piece was missing,
a piece about **as big as an egg** !

Chaim was upset as he washed his hands.
He was upset as he ate his bread and drank
his tea.

"I must be even more careful with my
bread next time," said Chaim.

A few days went by, and Chaim came home from the bakery with another loaf of bread.

He ate his bread and drank his tea.

Then Chaim had an idea.

He wrapped his bread carefully and hung it from the ceiling with a thin, slippery piece of thread.

Now his bread was really safe.

Chaim smiled as he said *Shema* and went to sleep.

The next night, when Chaim came home
from work and opened the door —

He thought he heard a scurrying sound.

He thought he saw something run by.

He thought he saw the tip of a tail shake
like a scolding finger.

Chaim jumped on a chair, pulled his bread off
the slippery thread and saw that a piece was
missing, a piece about **as big as an egg**!

Chaim began to wonder about the missing bread. He was thinking as he washed his hands. He was thinking as he ate his bread. He was thinking as he drank his tea.

Finally Chaim said to himself, "Not all of my bread is meant for me to eat. Some belongs in Bubbe Hinda's mitzvah sack."

The next time Chaim was able to get bread, he went back to the old bakery.

The night was cold. The line was long. Chaim was very tired and very hungry. Finally, it was his turn to show his card and get his small loaf of bread.

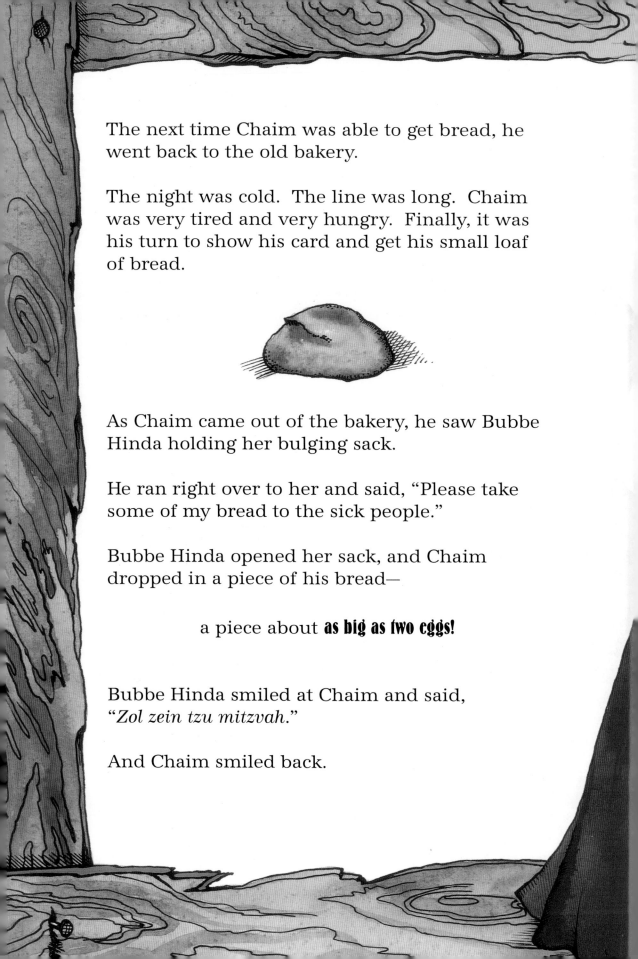

As Chaim came out of the bakery, he saw Bubbe Hinda holding her bulging sack.

He ran right over to her and said, "Please take some of my bread to the sick people."

Bubbe Hinda opened her sack, and Chaim dropped in a piece of his bread—

a piece about **as big as two eggs!**

Bubbe Hinda smiled at Chaim and said, "*Zol zein tzu mitzvah.*"

And Chaim smiled back.

When Chaim got home that night, he opened the door slowly and peeked inside.

He thought he felt something scurry across his foot.

He thought he saw something run outside.

He thought he saw the tip of a tail shake
    like a friendly hand waving good-bye.

And Chaim never saw a hint of
Bubbe Hinda's helper again!